UNICORN MOON

by Gale Cooper

E. P. DUTTON   NEW YORK

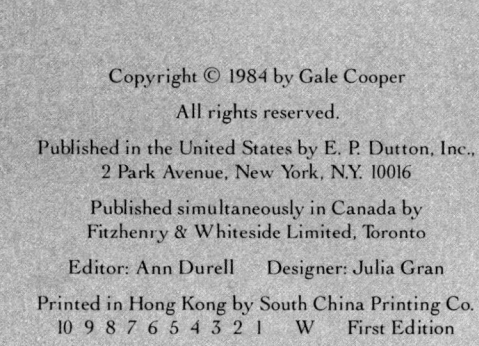

Published in the United States by E. P. Dutton, Inc.,
2 Park Avenue, New York, N.Y. 10016

Published simultaneously in Canada by
Fitzhenry & Whiteside Limited, Toronto

Editor: Ann Durell   Designer: Julia Gran

Printed in Hong Kong by South China Printing Co.
10 9 8 7 6 5 4 3 2 1   W   First Edition

LIBRARY OF CONGRESS CATALOGING IN PUBLICATION DATA

Cooper, Gale.
  Unicorn moon.

  Summary: A princess searches for the meaning
of true love, in order to break the spell over
a young man she sees constantly in her dreams.
  [1. Fairy tales.   2. Dreams—Fiction]   I. Title.
PZ8.C79Un   1984   [Fic]   84-1634
ISBN 0-525-44148-4

for Rose and Ira Cooper

with special thanks to Rudy Vaca, Michael Crichton,
Mary Byrd, Rita Bronowski, Ann Durell, Riki Levinson,
Eva Nichols, Joe Carpenter, Robert Dinnerman,
Frank Nightengale, Mandell Weiss, Bill Rivers,
Dianne Holly, and Roberta Yuen

One afternoon a young princess looked up at the sky and noticed the round day-moon. It was chalk white and flat, against a blue, cloudless sky.

That night the wind blew through pine branches whispering, "Alone, alone. Your queen mother is dead, your king father is at war, and you are alone, alone."

She slept and dreamed. In a dark land, she saw a pale and beautiful young man riding a steed with one silver horn. Through brilliant crystal snow they raced, following three huge hounds white as bleached bones. The dogs seized a doe, and her dying cry pierced the night.

In the echoing silence, the princess heard the young man's song:

> I am a lonely hunter,
> My fate lies in your heart.
> Dream the dream
> That sets me free,
> And we will never part.

He rode toward her, saying in a deeply sad voice, "This is the land of Unicorn Moon. Here the moon's pale glow is our only light, and the unicorn runs in endless hunt with the wild hounds."

She gazed at him longingly. "Who are you?" she asked.

But before he could answer, the dream came to an end.

The next night, the dream returned. Again the young man rode toward her, singing:

> I am a lonely hunter,
> My fate lies in your heart.
> Dream the dream
> That sets me free,
> And we will never part.

At his side raced the three white hounds; the unicorn's horn shone silver in the gloom.

He spoke with urgent despair. "Come! Ride with me and hunt with the hounds of Unicorn Moon."

The princess longed to be with him. But she cried, "I cannot hunt and kill innocent deer. Do not ask that of me."

She turned her head, and her pillow brushed her face. The dream was gone.

The princess now refused to leave her bed. She would not eat or drink, and the whole castle was filled with concern for her.

The royal magician was summoned to her side. He said, "Your Highness, I believe that you are under a cunning spell. Let me hang around your neck this crystal of amethyst and quartz. It will end the enchanted dream."

But she answered, "Take it away. If a spell has been cast, I will leave this world and live in exile. I refuse your cure."

She fell asleep and returned a third time to the land of Unicorn Moon. But she did not see the young man. Instead a terrible hag appeared. A snake was coiled around her waist, and her eyes were deep as a skull's.

"Abandon your hopes," she said. "He is under my spell, and you can never free him."

As the princess stood crying, the dream became mist, and the mist became morning.

News of her distress reached her father, the king, and he hastened back to the castle.

"Give up this dream," he commanded, "and garments of gold will be woven for you and stitched with fine pearls and gems. You will have a castle of your own, a stable of horses, and chests filled with coins."

But she answered, "I would gladly give up all your royal treasures to be with the one in my dreams."

And she eagerly returned to sleep and to the land of Unicorn Moon. The youth sat by a lake flat as glass, the unicorn and hounds nearby.

He beckoned to her and said softly, "Come to me, Princess, and let the unicorn carry us off into the long night."

Her heart filled with love, and she rushed toward him. But the faster she ran, the slower she moved. And his face changed. Tears ran down his cheeks.

Finally he whispered, "For this moment, your love gives me the strength to speak the truth. I am locked in this dream by a spell cast by the hag. There is a riddle you must solve to free me. If you can discover what true love is, the spell will be broken. If you fail, then we both will be lost forever in the land of Unicorn Moon."

Then through the darkness echoed the laughter of the hag, ugly, vicious and cruel. "Far wiser than you have failed to find the answer to this riddle. And you will fail too."

Then the princess stood alone with the wind blowing bitter and cold. And she awoke trembling and in fear.

A search began throughout the land to solve the riddle of true love. For by the king's decree, three hundred gold coins were the reward for the answer.

First came a poor couple, hoping for the prize. "True love is contentment," they said. "It is a belly full of food, the warmth of the hearth, and a friend by the side."

So she dreamed that night of a warm fire and of the young man near its glow. But the flames rose so high that she was afraid.

The hag called out, "If you want the warmth of the fire, you must risk the burn. The riddle is unanswered." And her laughter was terrible to hear.

Next came a teacher, looking solemn and wise. "The answer to the riddle is that there is no answer. True love is a fancy made up by storytellers."

She took this answer into her dream. "True love does not exist," she told the young man. But when their eyes met, they knew the answer was false.

"Princess, you will dream out all your days long before you find the answer you seek," crooned the hag's voice. "The youth is mine." And the hounds howled in the cold, pale light of Unicorn Moon.

Then came a soldier with a passion for gold in his eyes. He said, "True love is the power that destroys all who stand in its way." And he gave her a dagger to prove his answer was right.

Into her dreams she carried the weapon and tried to kill the hag. But as she stabbed, the witch laughed, and the blade cut only air.

When the princess awoke, she was white as the dead, and her eyes were empty and dull. Throughout the land a weeping arose, for all believed she was lost.

To her then came an old, old man. "I am a simple person," he said. "I cannot solve the riddle for you, because each walks his own path to find truth. But I can give you a gift. Take this long silver thread. Tie one end to your bedpost and hold the other in your hand. It will make a bridge between waking and sleeping and perhaps you can find the way to understand love."

When time came for sleep, she grasped the long thread, but her heart was filled with doubt. Then in the dream she ran across a vast plain and saw her love far away.

Suddenly she knew that she could not leave again. And she called, "I will give you my life. I will never awake. We will always remain together."

He ran to her calling, "Dear one, you will be mine forever."

But as he neared her, in his eyes she saw endless night. As her hand grasped his, she felt only mist.

And she cried out, "You are only a dream. But now I know what true love is."

True love is the fire of becoming one.
True love is the ice of becoming two.
But though the souls become united,
To the self each must stay true.

"I love you" were her farewell words. "But I must save myself." And she pulled on the silver string. The young man's voice echoed, "I love you. That is why I must now save myself."

As she drifted swiftly away, the cold, cold breath of the hounds of Unicorn Moon rushed around her heels. The unicorn reared and uttered a scream, and the dream was no longer there.

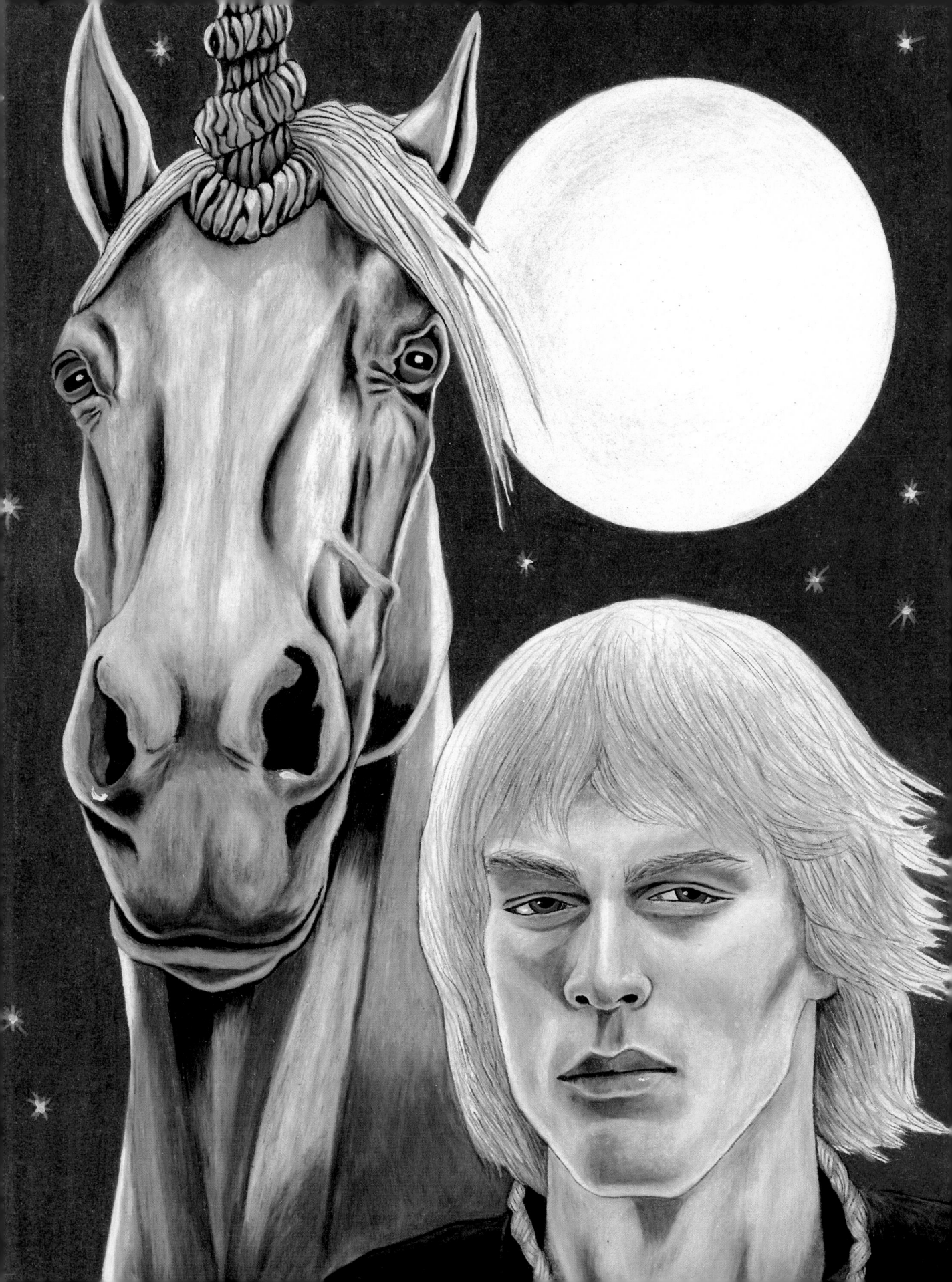

And when she awoke in brilliant sunlight, at the edge of her bed sat the young man.

"For me, you walked to the edge of death, but chose to live," he said. "You refused to stay in a sad dream, even for a promise of love. When you saved yourself, you saved me. The hag's spell is broken."

And their kiss was the seal of the living, and their love was the love of life.